Moon Was Tired of Walking on Air

Natalia M. Belting

Art by
Will Hillenbrand

Houghton Mifflin Company
Boston 1992

To Paul and Daniel Rundle, their cousins, Kenzie and
Brad Rundle, and to Emily Fox, who for years has listened
to my stories before they ever saw print.

—N.M.B.

To Ken & Sylvia Marantz and Anne Miotke

—W.H.

Library of Congress Cataloging-in-Publication Data

Belting, Natalia Maree, 1915–
  Moon was tired of walking on air : origin myths of South American
Indians / Natalia M. Belting : illustrated by Will Hillenbrand.
    p. cm.
  Summary: A collection of myths of various South American Indian
tribes, explaining the natural world.
  ISBN 0-395-53806-8
  1. Indians of South America—Legends. [1. Indians of South
America—Legends. 2. Nature—Folklore.] I. Hillenbrand, Will,
ill. II. Title.
F2230.1.F6B46 1992   91-20946
398.2′098—dc20   CIP
              AC

Text copyright © 1992 by Natalia M. Belting
Illustrations copyright © 1992 by Will Hillenbrand

Printed in the United States of America

HOR 10 9 8 7 6 5 4 3 2 1

Contents

PERU

Campas

BOLIVIA

BRAZIL

Apanyekra

Ramkokamekra

Cayapo

Tapirapé

Bororo

Toba

Chorote

PARAGUAY

ARGENTINA

Tehuelces

TIERRA DEL FUEGO

Selkam

Introduction

The Ancestors scattered over the earth. They built
homes beyond the south, where the land ends in
the frozen sea and the wind blows off the ice
without ceasing. They built toward the north and
the east on the grasslands that stretch to the edge
of the sky. They went farther north and built on the
high sandy table lands, in the thorny bush country
along streams flowing into the river that the white
man, when he saw it, called the Amazon. They
lived toward the west in the mountain foothills, in
deep forests near rocky gorges filled with noisy,
rushing water.

They looked at the earth and wondered at the
sky, and the animals, the birds and the fishes. How
was the earth made? How did Sun and Moon, how
did the stars, get into the sky? Where did they
themselves come from, and where had the animals
lived before? How was night made, and the
seasons? Why was Rainbow bent?

They wondered, dreamed, asked one another,
told their children what they knew, what they
learned: this is the way, they told them, that things
came to be.

Moon Was Tired of Walking on Air

A Myth of the Chorote Indians

Moon made the earth. "So," he told his wife, "we can have something to walk around on. I am tired of walking on air."

"Earth? What is earth?" she asked. "Whatever it is, you can't make it."

"I can, and I will," Moon said.

"Out of what?"

"Out of dust," he said, and took a handful from the air. He marked a square, spread the dust on it, wet it. "This will be the earth," he said.

Moon's wife looked. The dust was no longer dust. It was firm and hard. "It may be earth," she said, "but your foot is larger than your earth."

"Watch," Moon answered. "Grow," he said to the earth.

The earth grew. It spread in all directions. It was hard and flat. It was large enough for both of them to stand on.

"You were right," Moon's wife said. "It will be good to walk about with something solid under our feet."

Moon's children liked the earth. They played on it. They ran on it, and they did not come to the edge of it.

Caragusta grass sprouted. Its spiny leaves stretched out over the earth, and its tall thistles grew up in thick clumps.

"We cannot eat caragusta grass," Moon said. "I will burn some off, make a field, and plant seeds."

"Burn?" his wife asked. "What is burn? What are seeds?"

"Watch," Moon said. He pointed his finger. Fire came and burned the grass. He pointed again; a field was cleared and ready for planting. He curled up his fingers, then opened them. A seed lay in his palm. He planted it, sprinkled it with water.

At once a sprout broke through the earth. Before Moon could take a step, vines were spreading over the ground.

Moon and his wife watched. The vines budded and flowered; fruit formed. By evening the field was covered with ripe squash.

Moon picked a squash. His wife cut it open; they tasted it. "This is good," they said.

Then Moon cleared other fields, planted one seed in each. All that grows on the earth, Moon planted.

The Traveling Sky Baskets

A Myth of the Apanyekra Indians

One morning, at the beginning of time,
after the ancestors had come on earth,
Pud — Sun — and Pudlere — Moon — went up to the sky. They left
the house they had built among the palm trees and the fields they had
cleared and planted and harvested.

"The earth has changed," Pud said.

"Yes," Pudlere agreed. "It is too crowded."

"If we are going to live in the sky," Pud said, "we will need to make
paths to follow. I need one for the day."

"I will need one for the night," Pudlere said.

But the first day they were in the sky, Pud burned the earth. The streams
boiled up, the grass withered, and the armadillos dug deeper and deeper to
get away from the heat.

The first night Pudlere crossed the sky, the water that had not boiled
away froze; frost covered the burned grass, and the armadillos shivered in
their burrows.

"This will not do," Pud said.

"It will not do at all," Pudlere said.

"We need baskets," Pud said.

"Traveling baskets with lids," Pudlere added.

They wove their baskets, tried them out, liked them. Pud did not burn
the earth; Pudlere did not freeze it. To this day, Sun and Moon still cross
the sky in their traveling baskets. With lids.

What Happened When Fox
Opened the Bottle Tree

A Myth of the Chorote Indians

Fox, wandering about,
Came to the bottle tree
Where the Master of Fishes
Kept them and the earth's waters
Pent up for himself.

Fox looked at the trunk
Swollen with water,
With spines like a cactus
Running the length of it,
And a door cut into it.

He found the key
Where the Master of Fishes
Had hid it under a rock,
Unlocked the door,
Let the waters out
And the fish.

Fox ran.
The waters followed him,
Became rivers filled with fish.
He ran this way and that,
Jumped from ledge to rocky ledge
Down between the hills,
Trotted through the pampas,
The grassy meadows,
Dodged in and out among the palm trees.

Fox marked the course of the rivers,
Let loose the fishes for man.

Daughter of Rain

A Myth of the Cayapo Indians

There was a time when the people had no fields and grew no crops to feed themselves. There were no fruits or nuts growing wild. There were no animals to hunt, or birds, or fish. There was nothing to eat save lizards and palm leaves and the soft wood from fallen trees.

Mornings, Takako wandered about beyond the village, looking. He looked at the flat-topped hills rising out of the haze beyond the sandy plain. He looked at the scattered palms brushing their branches across the sky.

One morning he heard crying. He saw a young girl curled in the shade of a dwarf palm. She was not a village girl. She was ugly. Her black hair was long and tangled; her skin was pale. There was no paint on her arms or legs; there was no paint on her face; and tears stained her cheeks.

"Who are you?" Takako asked.

"I am Nyo-bog-ti, Great Light," she said. "I am the daughter of Rain."

"What are you doing down here? Why don't you go home?"

"I quarreled with my mother, and she struck me. I ran away. I don't want to go back."

"I suppose," Takako said, "I can take you to my house. I will have to hide you because you are ugly. You do not look like us."

"Please," Nyo-bog-ti answered. "I cannot stay here."

Takako went home and came again with a basket. "This is a basket for storing food," he said. "When we come to the village, you must get in before anyone sees you. I will put the basket up on the rafters under the roof. No one will know you are there."

"Yes," Great Light agreed, and so she came into the village, into the house, and no one knew she was there.

Nights, in the dark, while the family slept, Takako slid the cover off the basket, and Great Light came down from the rafters. They ate and talked. "No one knows you are here," Takako said.

So he thought. But one morning when he was gone from the house, his mother opened the basket.

"Come out," she said to the daughter of Rain, "come out so I can see you."

"No, I am ugly."

"Come out," she said again. "Well," she said when the girl had climbed out, "it is true you do not look like one of us, but I can take care of that. Sit down," she said, and pointed to the platform bed.

She cut the girl's hair, washed it, combed it. With red dye from the urucu palm, she painted broad stripes on Great Light's cheeks, her arms and legs, on her back and her chest and her stomach. She took the black juice of the genipa palm and painted thin lines next to the red stripes. She painted the

daughter of Rain as all the women painted themselves, as our women still paint themselves today.

Takako's father came home. "Why did you let the girl out of the basket?" he asked.

"You knew she was there?"

"I knew, but she is ugly. She does not look like one of us."

"Look at her," his wife said. "She is not ugly now."

He looked. "No, she is not ugly any longer," he said.

"She looks like one of us," his wife said. "She is one of us."

Takako came home. "She is beautiful," he said to his mother. "You are beautiful," he said to Nyo-bog-ti. "Will you marry me?"

"Yes," she said, and they were married.

The day came when she was tired of eating lizards and palm leaves and the soft wood of fallen trees. "Up in the sky," she said, "there are delicious things to eat. Sweet potatoes and manioc and beans. There are peanuts and cashews and palm nuts. There are turtles and ducks and armadillos."

"Can you get some of these for us?" Takako asked.

"Yes," she answered. They went out of the village. "There," she said, "that palm which strikes the sky with its branches, bend it down."

Takako bent the palm down and held it while his wife seated herself on a branch. He let the tree go. It sprang back, straightened itself, and threw Nyo-bog-ti into the sky.

Takako sat down; he waited; mid-day came; it was hot. "My wife has left me," he thought. "She is not coming back." He stood up. He heard his wife's voice behind him. He turned.

"Here I am," she said. "My father is coming, and my mother and my sisters."

Rain, whose name is Beb-gob-ro-ro-ti, came down. Sky, Great Light's mother, whose name is Ha, came down. Her sisters came. They brought baskets filled with crops that grew in the sky.

"These are for you and your village," Rain said. "Plant the seeds and the roots and they will grow for you as they do for us. But," he said to Takako, "treat your wife, my daughter, as a woman should be treated. I will see you if you beat her, and I will punish you."

So the villagers took the seeds and the roots and planted them. Beb-gob-ro-ro-ti watched, watered the crops as they needed it, sent animals down from the sky, and filled the rivers with fish. And the villagers no longer ate lizards and palm leaves and the soft wood from fallen trees.

Why Rainbow Is Bent

A Myth of the Selkam Indians

Akainik, Rainbow, that is,
Lived at Land's End
Where South ruled,
The home of the winds, of the rain,
A land of peat swamps,
Ice-sheeted mountains,
And summer rivers running off tongues of ice.

It happened that South,
Enamored, in love, with North's daughter,
Stole her away.

But North came after her,
Forced South to do battle.
They wrestled,
And their men wrestled,
Man against man.

South won,
But Akainik was thrown,
  Flung down,
   Pinned, his back injured.

   Since that day
   Rainbow has walked
Bent over,
Head down,
Like an old man.

Why Sun Has a Headdress and Moon Has None

A Myth of the Ramkokamekra Indians

One morning when Sun and Moon lived together on earth, Pud went out before Pudlere woke. Fish splashed in the river, kingfishers darted after them, herons skimmed the water. Parakeets flew in and out among the tree tops, and the plumed woodpeckers worked on the thorny trunks of the palms.

"I wish," Pud — Sun — said to the woodpeckers, "I had a headdress like yours."

"We will give you one," the birds answered, and they tossed it to him. "Don't drop it."

It was red, and it twisted in the air as it fell. Pud turned this way and that, his hands out. He caught the headdress.

It was hot, hot as fire. Pud tossed it from one hand to the other until it cooled.

"It is beautiful," he said, and he took it home.

"I want one like it," Pudlere — Moon — said when he saw it.

Pud and Pudlere went out to the palm forest.

"I want a headdress like the one you gave my friend Pud," Pudlere told the woodpeckers.

"We have one we can give you," they answered, "but it is the only one we have." They tossed it to him. "Don't drop it," they said.

"Let me catch it for you," Pud said.

"It is mine," Pudlere answered. "I can catch it."

But he dropped it. It burned his hands, and he dropped it. It set the bamboo on fire and the palm trees. It set fire to the grass, and the fires burned to the edge of the earth. The birds and the animals fled.

Pud and Pudlere went back to their homes in the sky, but to this day Sun has a headdress, the gift of the plumed woodpeckers, and Moon has none.

When Orekeke Wrestled Tornado

A Myth of the Teheulces Indians

Orekeke stood where his house had stood. It was gone,
blown away. All the houses were gone. Tornado, Shamej Jooshe,
had torn up the house poles, spread the stitched guanaco hides —
the walls and the roofs — across the califate bush and the wild holly.
"This time," his sister said, "he did not get any of us. We saw him
coming and we hid."

"He will come back unless we stop him."

"How?" Orekeke's brother asked. "We do not even know
where he lives."

"He lives in a cave in the mountains," Kai, the medicine
man, answered.

"I saw him when I was a young man."

"You went to Tornado's cave?"

"His mother's cave. She owns the healing powers, and she gives them
only to those who go to her for them."

"I will go," Orekeke said. "I will ask for the powers. And I will deal with
Tornado."

He fastened on his leggings, slid his feet into moccasins. He pulled his
pointed hood, fur-lined, down over his ears and his forehead. He belted his
guanaco hide mantle close to his waist, its fur next to his skin. He drew it
up on his shoulders that he might cover his face against the wind. And he
set out.

Day after day he walked; however he turned, whichever direction, he
walked into the wind. It swept yellow-gray dust over him, burned his skin
wherever it could. He crossed the flatlands strewn with rock; he made his
way among bushes armed with thorns and around wind-whipped, ice-shored
lagoons. He took the guanacos' path up mountains and through forests of
evergreen beech to the cave of the mother of winds.

He went in, took off his mantle and hood, and made himself one of the shadows. He crept behind Tornado where he sat, seized him by his long hair.

They wrestled. Wrestled the length of the cave. Wrestled at the mouth of the cave. Tornado was strong. Orekeke was quick. He twisted and turned, kept his head and his hair out of reach.

Tornado tired, grew weak and fell. He did not get up.

Orekeke straightened, stood. "Stay away from us," he said. "If you do not, I will come back. I will throw you so you will never get up."

He belted his mantle about him, put on his hood, and waited a moment at the mouth of the cave. He felt, but did not see, Tornado's mother, the mother of winds, touch him. He knew the moment she gave him the power to heal.

Orekeke went back to his village. He became a worker of wonders, a shaman, a medicine man. And to this day, though the winds blow through the land, swirl around the village night and day, Tornado has never come back.

Ghosts and Souls

A Myth of the Tapirapé Indians

Ghosts of the new dead
Find homes in old,
Abandoned villages;
But when they are cold,
They come back in the dark
To warm themselves by the fires of the living.

Souls, when the ghosts
Are gone from the dead,
Enter the bodies of animals.

Frogs have the souls of chiefs,
And pigeons, the souls of ordinary men.
Pacas, the small, striped, gnawing animals
That are everywhere,
Have women's souls.

The souls of shamans,
    the magic-workers, medicine men,
Even the souls of shamans
    who cause death,
Join Kanawana, Thunder,
Where he lives with the
    white-haired topu.
Small beings, they travel in canoes
Made of gourds cut in half.
    The sound of their paddling
Is the noise of a storm,
Their hunting arrows let loose,
The flash of lightning.

Fox and the Parakeet Women

A Myth of the Chorote Indians

Kixwet — Fox — while going about, found men without wives. "There are no women," the men told him.

"I will get some for you," Fox said. He called Kililik — Sparrow Hawk.

"You are a handsome fellow," Fox said.

"Killy," Sparrow Hawk agreed. "I am."

"Smallest of all the hawks," Fox said.

"But just the right size for me."

"The right size for the parakeet women," Fox said. "I need them down here for the men who have no wives. Go to the sky where they live. Persuade them to come back with you."

"Killy," Sparrow Hawk said. "I will do it. They will admire my looks. They will come because they will not be able to resist me."

He was right. "What a handsome person you are," the parakeet women said when they saw him. "There is no one so handsome as you."

"Come down to earth and visit me," he said.

"But how will we get down?" they asked. "We have wings, but we cannot fly that far."

"There is a tree that grows in the savanna, the grasslands, below," Kililik said. "Its branches brush the sky. Come, I will show you. You can fly down from one branch to another."

So the parakeet women came down from the sky; they perched in the caragusta thicket;

they watched Sparrow Hawk hovering, catching insects in the air. And while they were looking at Kililik, Fox cut down the tree. They heard it fall. "What shall we do?" they cried. "We cannot go home. We cannot fly that far."

"Stay here," Fox said. "I will show you the men who have no wives."

The men came. "Will you marry us?" they asked.

"Yes. If we cannot go back to the sky we must have husbands."

So the parakeet women married the men; they built houses for their husbands like parakeet nests. But they were not happy.

They went to Fox. "There is nothing to eat," they told him. "The men hunt and

bring back meat. But we do not eat meat. Make us like our husbands," they asked Fox.

"Go to sleep," Fox said, and they did.

He sprinkled earth on them. "Wake up," he said, and they did.

They looked at each other. "We are women," they said. "We are not parakeets any longer." They thanked Fox. "Now we can eat the same food our husbands eat."

But to this day our people build houses that look like parakeet nests, larger, of course, but the same shape and made the same way.

Worlds Above, Worlds Below

A Myth of the Toba Indians

There are worlds above the earth,
Worlds below.
The blue sky
And the white sky above it,
The yellow-green sky above the white
Are worlds: demons and spirits, animals
Dwell there . . .
Jaguar in one,
Big Fox in another,
Spider in the topmost sky.
And in the red sky
Above the yellow-green sky
Live the Ossasero birds, the rain makers.
The world below the earth is empty
Since the Ancestors came up.
(Other people may have come from the sky
But the Tobas came from the world
Below this world.)
The bottom-most world
Is crossed by the path the sun follows
From its setting at night
To its rising.

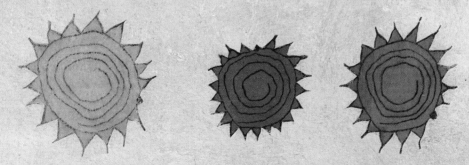

How Averiri Made the Night and the Seasons

A Myth of the Campas Indians

In the time before this time, when Averiri traveled about, there was the earth and the sky and the river. There were families and villages. But there was no night. There were no seasons. There was no season when the rains fell and the river flooded. There was no season when the earth and the air warmed and the river went back into its banks. There was no time when the sky grew dark.

Averiri came to his sister's house. His sister and the other women set out food. Their neighbors came and they feasted on meat stew, fish roasted in bamboo, and watermelon. When the eating was done, Averiri reached for his pipes — hollow reeds bound together. He blew into them and made music. He took the sounds of bats setting off to hunt and the screams of the macaws. He took the sounds of the tree frogs quaking and drumming, the howls of monkeys racing through the trees. He took the hum and clatter and whistle of forest insects, put words to the sounds, sang them. He played his pipes and sang. And with his music, Averiri made the night. He took the sounds of thunder crashing, of rain rattling and pounding, of the rising river throwing itself against its rocky banks; he took the soft sounds of feet sinking in wet sand and the plop of mud bubbling up, put words to the sounds, sang them. He played his pipes and sang. And with his music Averiri made the wet season.

He took the sounds of hot winds blowing through the palms and the sounds of fish sucking air as the waters went down; he took the thud of ripe fruit falling, the crackle of bamboo, the rustle of grass withering, put words to the sounds, sang them. He played his pipes and sang. And with his music Averiri made the dry season.

The night and the seasons, Averiri made with his music.

What Happened When Armadillo Dug a Hole in the Sky

A Myth of the Cayapo Indians

In the days before these days, the people lived in the sky. Everywhere there were trees — trees the women had to cut and clear, trees that sprouted among rows of sweet potatoes and pineapples and manioc, trees that had to be pulled like weeds.

A man out hunting one day came upon a giant armadillo. He reached for his club; before he could raise it, the armadillo had dug a hole and disappeared.

The hunter started digging; he dug all day, dug the next day, and the day after. Four days he dug in the burrow before he caught up to the armadillo. He reached for its tail.

The bottom of the burrow broke; the armadillo fell out of the sky, fell to the earth. The man looked down. "The earth is beautiful," he thought. "I must go down."

He went home. He told his wife, told the headmen, and all the villagers about the armadillo's hole in the sky. "I looked down," he said, "and saw grasslands everywhere. The trees stand in groves on the edge of the meadows. There are palm trees, the buriti palm and the tucum palm, the peach palm and the feather palm, all with fruits to eat. But the women will not have to cut them down to get fields for their crops."

"Is there water?" the headmen asked.

"I saw a river, clear and blue, full of fish, and with white flowers floating on it."

The headmen consulted together. They spoke to the villagers. They decided.

"We shall go down to the earth," they said, "and see if it is better for living."

"How?" the villagers asked.

"We will use a rope," the headmen answered. "Bring your belts and your bracelets and your anklets. We will tie them together for a rope."

They made the rope, let it down through the hole. But it was not long enough. They made a second rope, and a third. Each was too short. But the fourth rope, when they let it down, touched the earth, dragged on the ground.

A headman climbed down and tied the rope to a tree trunk.

The villagers climbed down — the children and their parents, even the parents' parents. A few villagers did not. "We want to think about it," they said.

"You are afraid," a boy shouted up to them. He grabbed the rope where it was tied to the tree and cut it.

The villagers who waited to think are still in the sky. They are the stars. And the people who came down had no way to return. They are the Ancestors.

The Ancestors Are All Around Us

A Myth of the Selkam Indians

Kenos, son of Kehacomh — South — and of Soonh-Woman — Heaven —
came to the earth when it was empty. He arranged the land and the
mountains and the sea. He set the Ancestors down in tribes and taught
them to speak.

He lived long and grew tired. His three friends who had come with him
also grew old and tired. They lay down; for a great while they could not
sleep. Sleep, when it came, did them no good. They woke, still tired, still
old.

"It may be," Kenos said, "if we go up north we will find a place where
sleep has more power."

The four of them set out for the north, taking the trail through the beech
forests that edged the mountain glaciers. They crossed peat bogs and icy
streams. They dragged themselves through the scrub and the grass, bent
over, limping as the aged do.

They came at last, as the weather warmed, to rolling hills covered with
buttercups and carpeted with daisies. They came to the villages of the north.

"Wrap us in mantles," Kenos told the villagers. "Prepare us for burial."

It was done. The villagers wrapped them in mantles of guanaco fur and
laid them on the ground. The people watched and mourned as they did for
friends who had died. Kenos and his companions did not move,

nor breathe. Night came, and another night, another, and one more after that.

Kenos stirred. His companions stirred. They moved their lips, they spoke, they sat up. They stood. They washed themselves in the stream. They were young again and full of life.

After them the Ancestors, wherever they lived, did likewise. When they were old and tired, they wrapped their mantles about themselves and lay down as if they were dead. The families watched and mourned; the sleepers did not move or breathe. One night followed another until their sleep ended. They stirred; they spoke and stood up. They went, each of them, to Kenos.

"Wash us," they said. Kenos washed them. They were young again, healthy, full of vigor.

So the Ancestors lived, grew old and tired, slept and woke, were washed, and were young again. But those who wearied of so much sleeping and waking went to Kenos.

"We do not want to be young again," they told him.

Kenos transformed them, changed those who came to him who were tired of being young and growing old. Some became the winds. Some became birds — the great owl, the wood owl and the dark ground owl, the albatross, the bald buzzard, the cormorant and the duck — all the birds of the air.

Some became the squid, the whale, and the sea lion — the animals and fish of the sea. Some became the jaguar, the tucotuco, the fox, the bat, the armadillo — all the animals of the land. And some, when Kenos went back to live in the sky, went with him; they became the clouds and the stars.

Today, wherever we look, we can see the Ancestors.

How the Birds Got New Beaks and Men Got Teeth

A Myth of the Bororo Indians

The red macaw complained.

The yellow macaw complained.

The dark blue macaw complained.

"There is all that fruit on the palm trees," they said, "and we cannot eat it. Our beaks are not strong enough."

They flew to Meri — Sun — in the village. They told him, "Our beaks are not strong enough to open the palm nuts."

"Go to the village plaza," he said. "Call all the birds. Tell them I will give new beaks to all who ask."

The birds came, flew down from the flat-topped hills, flew out of the palm forests and the grasslands, flew up from the river. The birds came to the plaza. The villagers came too.

The red macaw stood before Meri. Meri took up a piece of white quartz, shaped it into a beak, and fitted it on the red macaw.

"Try it," Meri said.

The red macaw held a palm nut between his feet, struck it, cracked it open. "It is a good beak," he said. "Thank you."

The yellow macaw stood before Meri. Meri took up a piece of black

quartz, shaped it into a beak, polished it, fitted it on the yellow macaw.

"Try it," he said.

The yellow macaw opened a palm nut. "It is a good beak," he said. "Thank you."

The dark blue macaw flew down and stood before Meri. Meri took up a second piece of black quartz, a large piece, shaped it into a beak, polished it, fitted it onto the dark blue macaw. "Try it on this fruit of the tucum palm," he said. "If you can open it, you can open any palm nut."

The dark blue macaw held the tucum palm nut between his feet, struck it, opened it. "Good," he said. "Thank you." And he flew off.

The parrots came; Meri made them new beaks of quartz, smaller but strong.

Hummingbird flew down and told Meri, "My beak is too short."

Meri took a long thorn from the tucum palm, polished it, fitted Hummingbird with it. "Here," he said, "drink from this." He held out a yellow flower, long-necked like a squash blossom. Hummingbird drank its nectar.

"Thank you," he said. "It is a fine beak."

Kingfisher came, and heron and ibis. "Our beaks are no good for fishing," they said. Meri fashioned new beaks — hunting spears — of palm thorns and fitted them. He made beaks of all shapes and kinds and gave the birds new beaks, good beaks.

The village chief came to Meri. "Our mouths are no better for eating than the mouths of turtles," he said.

"What you need," Meri said, "are teeth." He raked up a pile of white stones, shaped them,

polished them, fitted them in the chief's mouth.

The chief cut a slice of pineapple and chewed it.
"This is much better, very much better. Thank you."

Meri gave all the villagers teeth. Then he said,
"I think you need fingernails and toenails, hard
nails like the birds and animals have, but not so
long or so pointed."

"Yes," the villagers agreed, "we need
fingernails and toenails."

So Meri, before the day was over, fitted
the villagers with fingernails and
toenails, making them of thin slices
of quartz, shaped and polished.